This Book Belongs To:

_____

A NOTE TO PARENTS

All children love to explore. Stories help to broaden children's natural inquisitiveness and imagination. *In Exploring We Go!*, Uniqua seeks a new, undiscovered place where no one has ever been. Along the way, she meets three friends who encourage and help her as they travel together far from home. Eventually, Uniqua finds out that what she was looking for was closer than she had ever dreamed.

As you read this story with your child, ask him if there are any special people he would want to take with him on a journey like Uniqua's. Would he want to sail a ship, as in the story, or rather fly in an airplane or rocket ship? Where would he choose to go?

This is a wonderful opportunity for you and your child to explore your own yard, nearby park, or other familiar place. Prepare a simple map that your child can follow (with your help, of course). Flowers, birds' nests, rock formations, or some interesting item that you secretly position so that it is easily found are just some of the things your child can "discover." Where did they come from? How did they get there? Also encourage your child to play-act his own explorer story. Besides being a great game, this will help your child become more aware of his surroundings and promote his imagination and creative abilities.

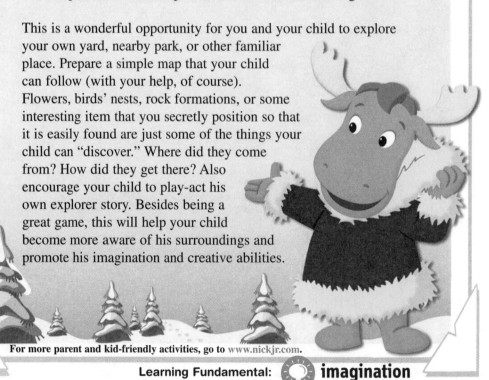

For more parent and kid-friendly activities, go to www.nickjr.com.

Learning Fundamental: **imagination**

EXPLORING WE GO!

Published by Scholastic Inc., 90 Old Sherman Turnpike, Danbury, CT 06816

SCHOLASTIC and associated logos are trademarks and/or registered trademarks of Scholastic Inc.

ISBN 0-7172-7795-X

Printed in the U.S.A.

3 1813 00385 3362

First Scholastic Printing, September 2005

EXPLORING WE GO!

by
Kitty Fross

**illustrated by
Gregg Schigiel**

SCHOLASTIC INC.

New York Toronto London Auckland Sydney
Mexico City New Delhi Hong Kong Buenos Aires

"What a perfect day for exploring," Uniqua thought happily. "Good thing I happen to be a Brave Explorer!" Walking towards her ship, Uniqua thought of all the places she could explore.

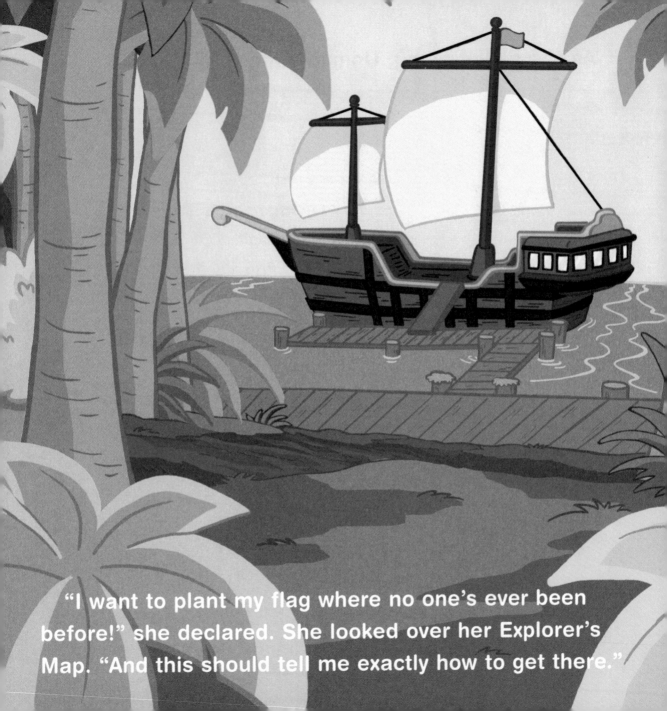

"I want to plant my flag where no one's ever been before!" she declared. She looked over her Explorer's Map. "And this should tell me exactly how to get there."

As she sailed along, Uniqua sang:

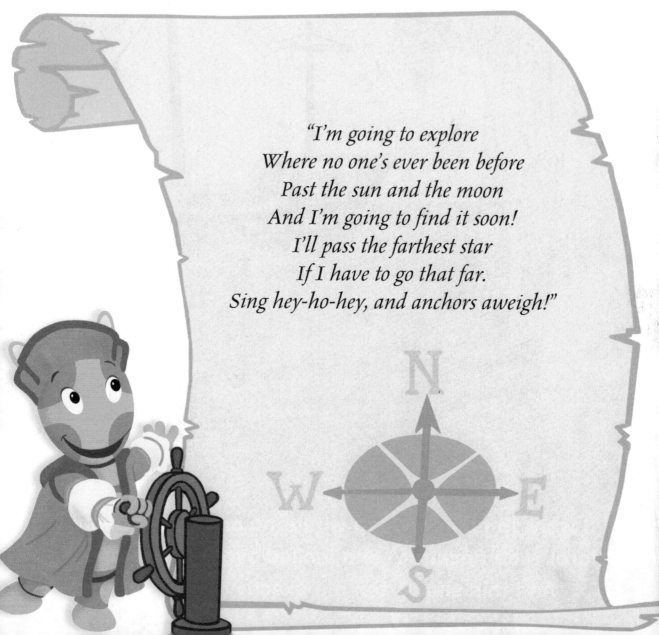

"I'm going to explore
Where no one's ever been before
Past the sun and the moon
And I'm going to find it soon!
I'll pass the farthest star
If I have to go that far.
Sing hey-ho-hey, and anchors aweigh!"

Uniqua sailed until the sun was behind her. Then she landed her ship on a beach in front of a thick jungle. "This jungle is so dark and wild, I doubt anyone's been here before!" Uniqua said.

Uniqua trekked in a short way and was about to plant her flag. "This was easy!" she said with a laugh.

"What was easy?" asked a voice out of nowhere.

"Who's there?" Uniqua called out.

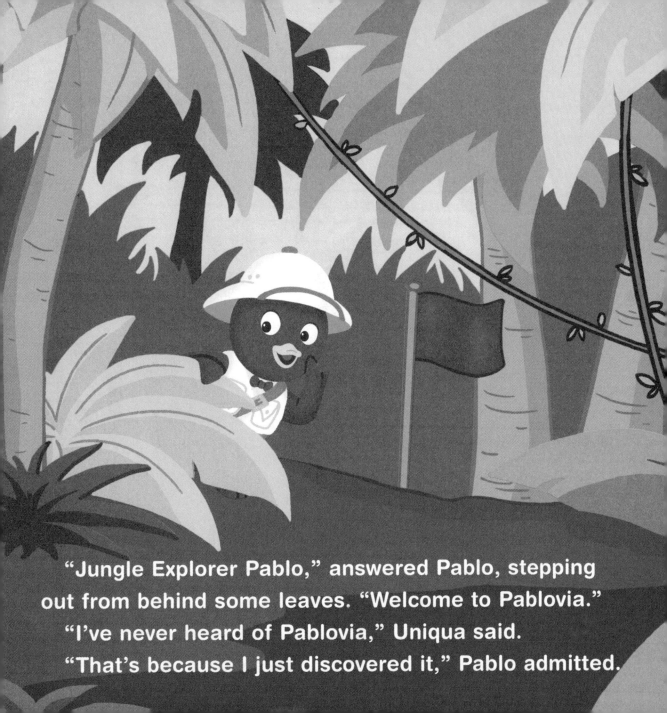

"Jungle Explorer Pablo," answered Pablo, stepping out from behind some leaves. "Welcome to Pablovia."

"I've never heard of Pablovia," Uniqua said.

"That's because I just discovered it," Pablo admitted.

"Well, I'm looking for a place where no one's ever been before. So I guess I'd better keep exploring," Uniqua said, turning to go back to her ship.

"I'll come with you," Pablo offered. "I'm pretty good at finding places no one's ever been before."

So Pablo and Uniqua set sail, singing:

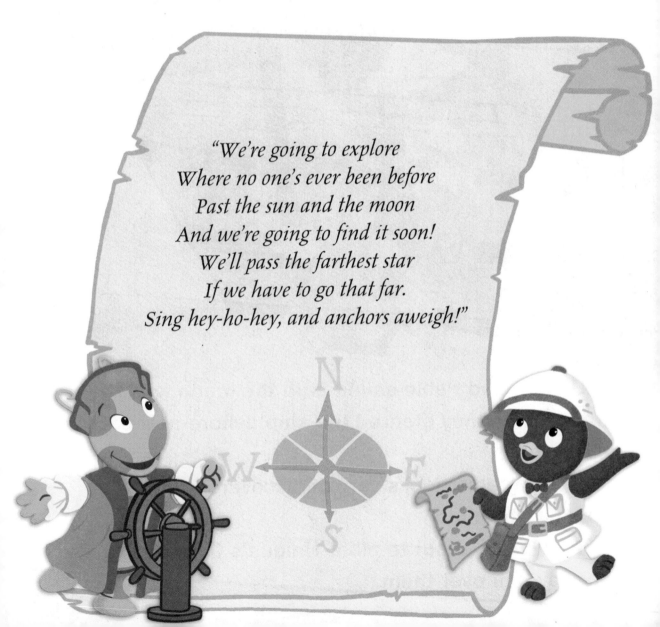

"We're going to explore
Where no one's ever been before
Past the sun and the moon
And we're going to find it soon!
We'll pass the farthest star
If we have to go that far.
Sing hey-ho-hey, and anchors aweigh!"

Uniqua and Pablo sailed until the moon was behind them. Then they steered the ship ashore at the edge of a glacier.

"This glacier looks very undiscovered to me!" Uniqua observed.

They were about to plant Uniqua's flag when a shadow fell over them.

"Does that look like a Snow Monster shadow to you?"
Pablo whispered nervously.

Ever so slowly, they turned around.

"Snow Monster!" Pablo screamed.

"Run for your life! Run!!!"

But before they could run, the Snow Monster took off his furry hood. "Wait, I'm not a Snow Monster," he explained. "I'm Glacier Explorer Tyrone."

"Have you already discovered this glacier?" Uniqua asked.

"I certainly have," Tyrone replied. "Welcome to Tyronia!"

Uniqua sighed. "I guess we'll have to keep looking for a place where no one's ever been before."

"I'll come with you." Tyrone offered. "With three Explorers, we'll probably find it three times as fast!"

Back on the ship, the three Explorers sang:

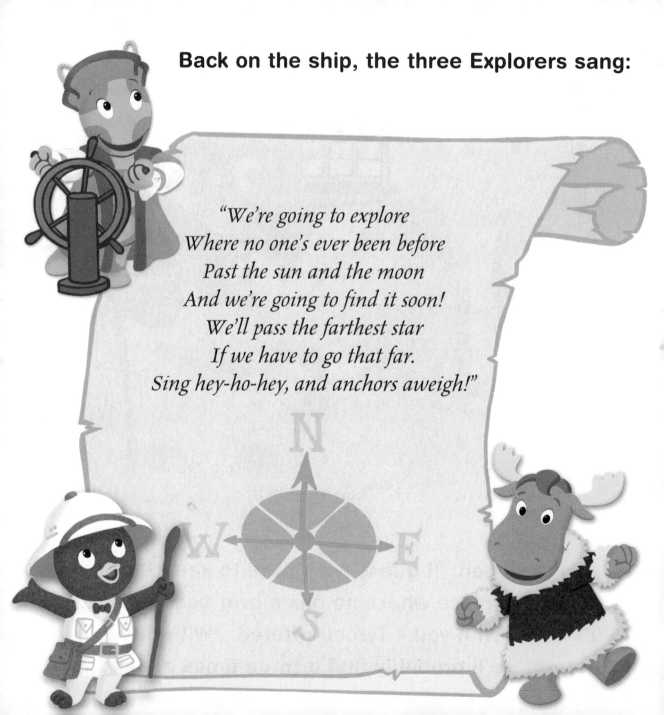

"We're going to explore
Where no one's ever been before
Past the sun and the moon
And we're going to find it soon!
We'll pass the farthest star
If we have to go that far.
Sing hey-ho-hey, and anchors aweigh!"

Before long, Tyrone spotted a distant island. "Explorer Uniqua!" he called out. "That looks like the Lost Island!"

"Is the Lost Island a place no one has ever been before?" Uniqua asked eagerly.

"No, it's just an island where I got lost once," Tyrone replied.

"Careful" Pablo warned. "There's Creeping Seaweed around the Lost Island!" "What does Creeping Seaweed do?" Uniqua asked.

"It creeps up on you, grabs your ship, and never lets go," Pablo explained.

As the Explorers talked, their boat drifted closer and closer to the Lost Island. Suddenly Uniqua looked over her shoulder. "Oh, no!" she gasped. "Creeping Seaweed! Now what do we do?"

"If only we had some soap," Tyrone mused. "We could make the ship slippery so the seaweed couldn't grab us."

"I have soap in my Explorer Bag!" Pablo shouted.

So Tyrone and Pablo soaped the sides of the ship while Uniqua steered away from the island.

"That was close," Uniqua breathed as they got underway again. "Good work, Explorer Pablo!"

"It's no big deal," Pablo said modestly. "Jungle Explorers always carry a bar of soap!"

The three Explorers sailed on until they passed the last star in the sky.

They trekked until they came to a desert. Then they hopped on camels and rode until they came to an oasis.

"This oasis is in the middle of nowhere," Uniqua exclaimed. "I'm sure no one's ever been here before!"

But before they could plant Uniqua's flag, a voice called out, "Hey, what are you doing on my oasis?"

"*Your* oasis?" Uniqua repeated.

"Sure. I'm Desert Explorer Tasha. And I discovered this oasis ten minutes ago," said Tasha haughtily.

"I guess we'll have to keep exploring," said Tyrone.

But Uniqua shook her head. "We've sailed to the end of the map. We're never going to find a place where no one's ever been before. I'm going home," she said.

"We'll come with you," Tasha said sympathetically.

So the four Explorers
returned to the ship. They
sailed and sailed until
they landed back
where Uniqua began.

After walking for a while, the group stopped to rest. "I'm sorry you didn't find what you were looking for," said Pablo.

"But at least you found three friends!" Tasha added brightly.

Just then, Uniqua noticed a huge flower hanging over her head. "Wow," she murmured. "I've never seen a flower like that! I guess I've never been in this clearing before."

"Neither have I," Tyrone said.

"Me, neither," said Pablo.

"I'd remember a flower like that!" Tasha agreed.

Uniqua's eyes began to gleam. "Wait . . . if *we've* never been here before, I bet *no one's* ever been here!"

As her friends nodded their agreement, Uniqua proudly planted her flag.

"Good work, Explorer Uniqua," Pablo cheered.

Uniqua and her friends sang one last time:

"We wanted to explore
Where no one's ever been before
We passed the sun and the moon,
We were sure we'd find it soon!
We passed the farthest star,
But didn't have to go that far.
'Cause it really wasn't hard –
It was in our own backyard!"

And then they had a snack.

Salt in His Shoes

Michael Jordan
In Pursuit of a Dream

BY DELORIS JORDAN WITH ROSLYN M. JORDAN

ILLUSTRATED BY KADIR NELSON

SIMON & SCHUSTER BOOKS FOR YOUNG READERS

NEW YORK LONDON TORONTO SYDNEY SINGAPORE

It is my hope that young readers and listeners will be motivated by this book to follow their dreams just as Michael followed his—by setting goals, working hard, and being dedicated. It's only when we do this that our dreams can and do come true. For that reason, I dedicate this book to the many children who are inclined to say "I can't," or "I wish I had talent," or "I wish I were gifted." To them I say, "You are gifted. You are talented and special. God has a plan for each of you; just believe in yourself and follow your dreams."
—D. J.

Every good and perfect gift comes from above. I give all praises to God for the gift to dream, the gift to believe, and the gift to be. I dedicate this book to all children who desire and are determined to mount up on wings as eagles and soar. By the grace of God you can fly. So just do it.
—R. M. J.

For Mom, Dad, Saliha, Amin, and Shedia
—K. N.

Acknowledgments

First, I thank my wonderful daughter and co-author, Roslyn, for her willingness to work with me, and for her inspiration and support. I am grateful for this opportunity to create with her—and grateful to her for showing her love, honesty, and courage.

Thanks also to Kevin Lewis, senior editor at Simon & Schuster Books for Young Readers for his commitment to this project and for making sure my voice was heard.

To Kadir Nelson for the imagination and great talent he brought to this project, thanks for the hard work.

To Amy Berkower, who worked with me to keep this project on time, thanks for the ideas and encouragement.

And finally to Michael, *Salt in His Shoes* is a tribute to him for not giving up, facing his challenges with confidence, and learning to never say "I can't." Thanks, son, for your support.

This book is also a tribute to Michael's siblings for the encouragement and support they have shown him along the way, as well as their continued efforts to fulfill their own goals.

SIMON & SCHUSTER BOOKS FOR YOUNG READERS

An imprint of Simon & Schuster Children's Publishing Division, 1230 Avenue of the Americas, New York, New York 10020. Text copyright © 2000 by Deloris Jordan with Roslyn M. Jordan. Illustrations copyright © 2000 Kadir Nelson. All rights reserved including the right of reproduction in whole or in part in any form. SIMON & SCHUSTER BOOKS FOR YOUNG READERS is a trademark of Simon & Schuster. Book designed by Paul Zakris. The text of this book is set in 14-point New Caledonia Semi Bold. The illustrations are rendered in oils. Manufactured in China.

10

Library of Congress Cataloging-in-Publication Data

Jordan, Deloris. Salt in his shoes / by Deloris Jordan with Roslyn Jordan; illustrated by Kadir Nelson. p. cm. Summary: Young Michael Jordan, who is smaller than the other players, learns that determination and hard work are more important than size when playing the game of basketball. ISBN 0-689-83371-7 1. Jordan, Michael, 1963– —Juvenile fiction. [1. Jordan, Michael, 1963– —Fiction. 2. Basketball—Fiction. 3. Size—Fiction.] I. Jordan, Deloris. II. Nelson, Kadir, ill. III. Title. PZ7.J76825Sal 2000 [E]—dc21 00-020539

0810 PXA

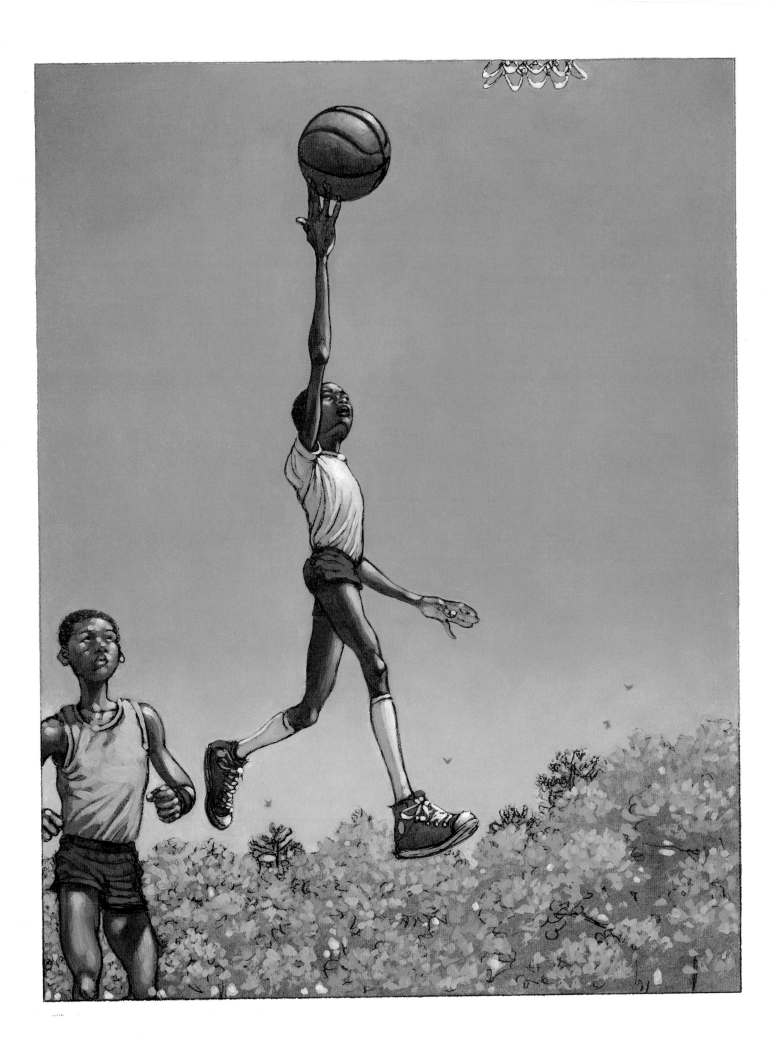

Michael loved to play basketball.

Every Saturday, he followed his older brothers, Larry and Ronnie, to the park, hoping that they would let him play. And if one of the guys who usually played with them didn't show, they always did. But there was one problem: his name was Mark, and he was the tallest boy on the court.

"What's the matter, Mikey, too short?" Mark flapped his arms in Michael's face.

"Over here!" shouted Larry. But when Michael threw the ball, Mark's long arms came out of nowhere and knocked the ball away. It flew into the hands of a player on Mark's team, he made the basket, and the game was over. Just like that.

"I am really sorry, guys. If I were taller that wouldn't have happened."
All the way home Michael apologized. Even though no one was mad at him.

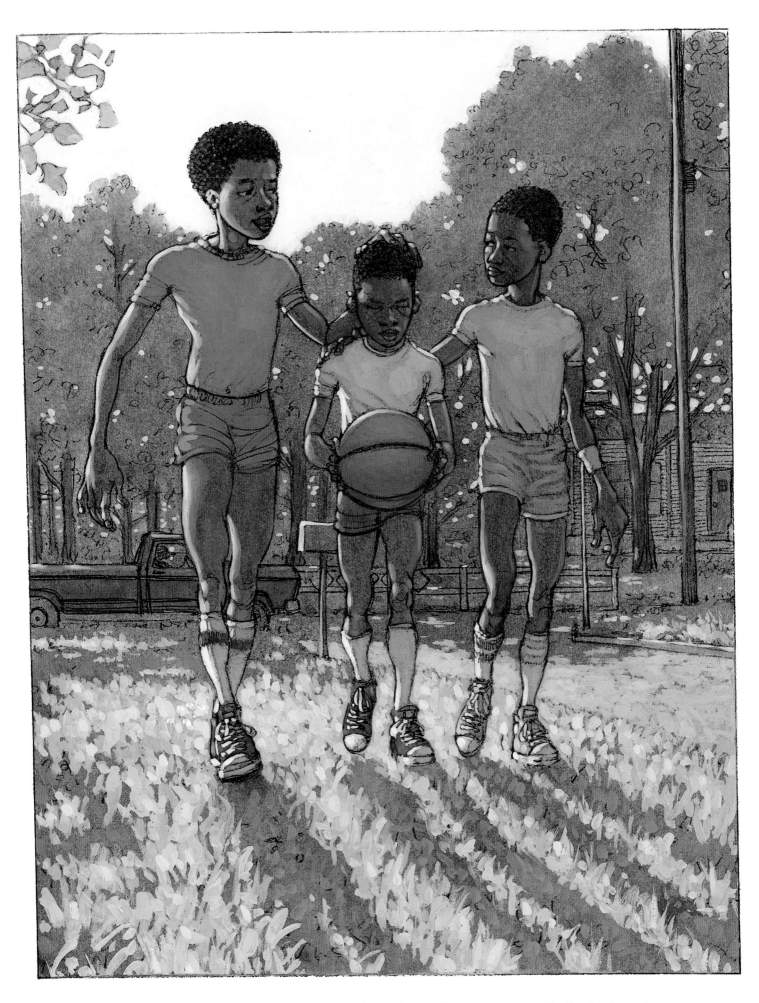

His oldest brother, Ronnie, tried to cheer him up. "Look, little brother, you played good today. Don't worry. We'll win the next time."

When they got home, Michael went into the kitchen where Mama was cooking dinner. He was still disappointed, and she could tell.

"You guys lost again today, huh?"

Michael nodded.

He sat quietly for a minute, then said, "Mama, how can I grow taller?"

Now, Mama knew the answer to a lot of questions, but this was a tough one. She thought for a moment as she sprinkled salt and pepper on the chicken she was making for dinner. Then she smiled, looked at Michael, and said, "Salt."

"Salt?" Michael looked at his mama.

"Salt in your shoes. We'll put salt in your shoes and say a prayer every night. Before you know it, you'll be taller!" she replied.

"Salt in my shoes?" Michael said quietly to himself. Surely Mama was teasing. He sat staring out of the window trying to figure out how salt was going to help him grow.

He noticed the rose bushes outside in Mama's garden. They had grown
high along the fence, and roses of all colors were blooming on the vines. He
thought to himself, *I remember when Mama first planted those bushes.*
Michael's face lit up. *If Mama knows how to make those rose bushes grow
taller, then maybe she's right. Maybe salt in my shoes really will help me grow.*

Growing more excited, Michael twirled around and started asking lots of
questions. "Mama, how long will it take? And how tall do you think I'll get?"

Smiling, Mama sat down next to him and explained. "In order for this
to work, the most important things you have to do are be patient and
listen to what I tell you, and say your prayers every night."

Listening carefully, Michael shook his head. "Okay, Mama, I'll be
patient. But what does saying my prayers have do with it?"

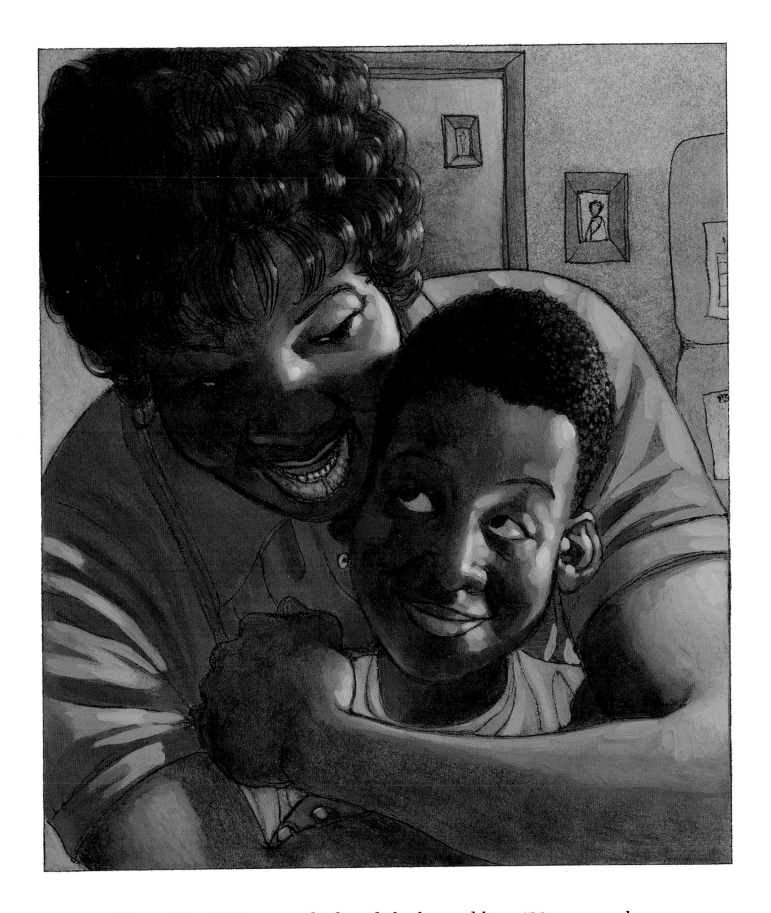

"Everything," Mama replied, and she hugged him. "Now go wash up and tell your brothers and sisters to get ready for dinner."

Michael dashed out of the kitchen, almost knocking over his father, who was walking in. "What's he up to now?" asked Daddy.

"Oh, the usual," laughed Mama, "chasing a dream."

Later during dinner, Mama noticed that Michael was barely eating anything. He was already daydreaming about being taller.

"Michael, first things first. You won't grow if you don't eat, especially your vegetables," Mama said.

"But I'm not really hungry," he said.

Raising her eyebrows, Mama gave him a stern look.

Slowly, Michael picked up his fork and began to eat. Minutes later his plate was clean and he was asking for more.

That evening at bedtime, Michael set his favorite game shoes on the floor next to the growth chart hanging on the wall. Then he put on his pajamas, said his prayers, and jumped into bed.

When Mama came in, Michael was fast asleep. By the look on his face
she could tell he was already playing basketball in his dreams.

Standing by his bed, Mama sprinkled salt in his shoes. Then she prayed quietly over him as she did all her children.

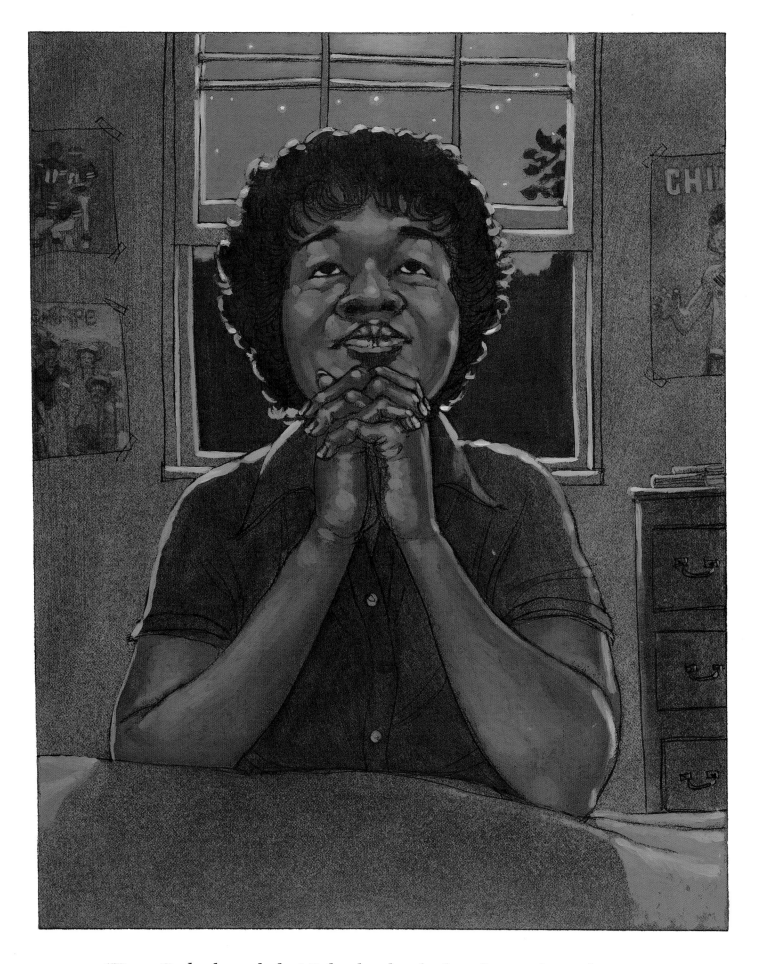

"Dear God, please help Michael to be the best he can be and to give his best in all that he does. And Lord, could You please make him just a little bit taller tomorrow than he is today? Thank You. Amen."

After that night Michael wore his favorite game shoes everywhere he went, even to church. And he stopped going to the park with his brothers on Saturdays. Instead he stayed home and practiced. He wanted to grow a few more inches before he went back to the park.

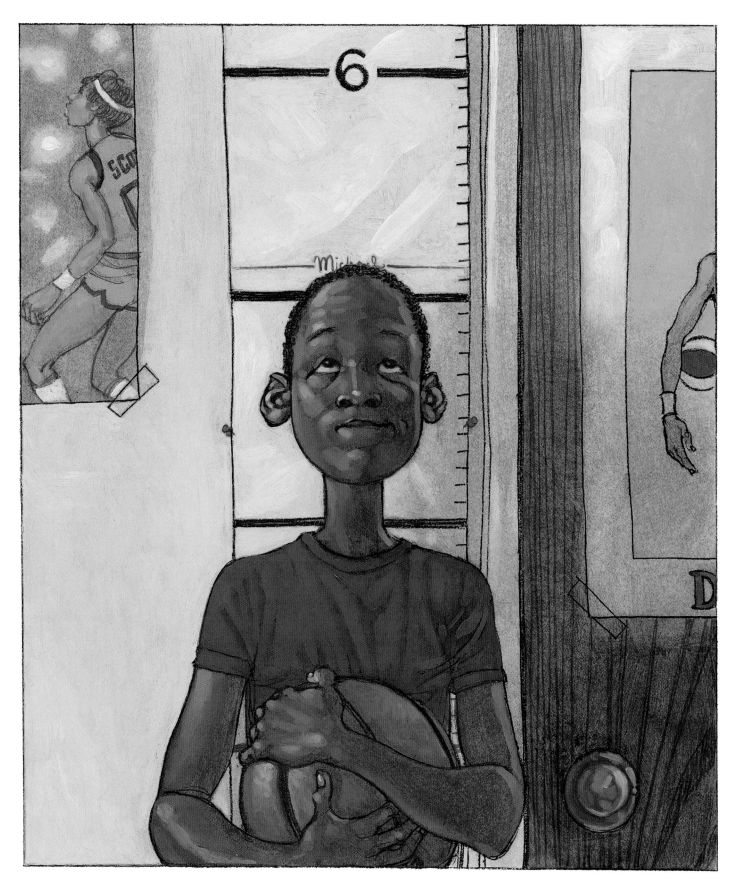

After two months of practicing and waiting patiently and praying, Michael stood next to the growth chart on his wall. Nothing. He hadn't grown an inch. He was disappointed, but he did not stop believing.

I've just got to give it time like Mama said, Michael thought to himself, and that's what he did.

Two more months of practicing went by and still nothing. Now Michael was becoming a little sad. Not only had he not grown one inch, but he also missed playing basketball with Larry and Ronnie. About the only thing he didn't miss was being picked on by Mark.

When the next Saturday came, his brothers tried to get Michael to go with them to the park, but he wouldn't budge. Mama had begun to worry. When she saw Michael sitting alone on the steps she said to Daddy, "Maybe you should go out and talk to him."

So Daddy went out and sat with Michael.

"What's wrong, son? You haven't gone to the park with your brothers for a while now. Are you okay?"

Michael didn't say anything at first. Then he looked at Daddy and said, "I thought I would at least be a few inches taller by now. I did everything Mama told me to do, but nothing's happened."

"Michael, why do you want to be taller?" Daddy asked.

"If I were taller I'd be a great player, and I could help our team win," Michael answered.

"But you *are* a great player, son. And you already have everything it takes to be a winner, right in here." Daddy tapped Michael on his chest. "Being taller may help you play a little better, but not as much as practice, determination, and giving your best will. Those are the things that make you a real winner."

Michael thought about what Daddy said for a minute. Then suddenly, he jumped up and took off.

"Where are you going?" Daddy yelled after him.

"I've got a game today, and I'm late," Michael yelled back.

When Michael reached the park the game had started. He sat on the bench hoping he would get a chance to play, and he did: The game was almost over and the score was tied when John, one of the guys on Michael's team, fell and hurt himself.

Here was Michael's chance.

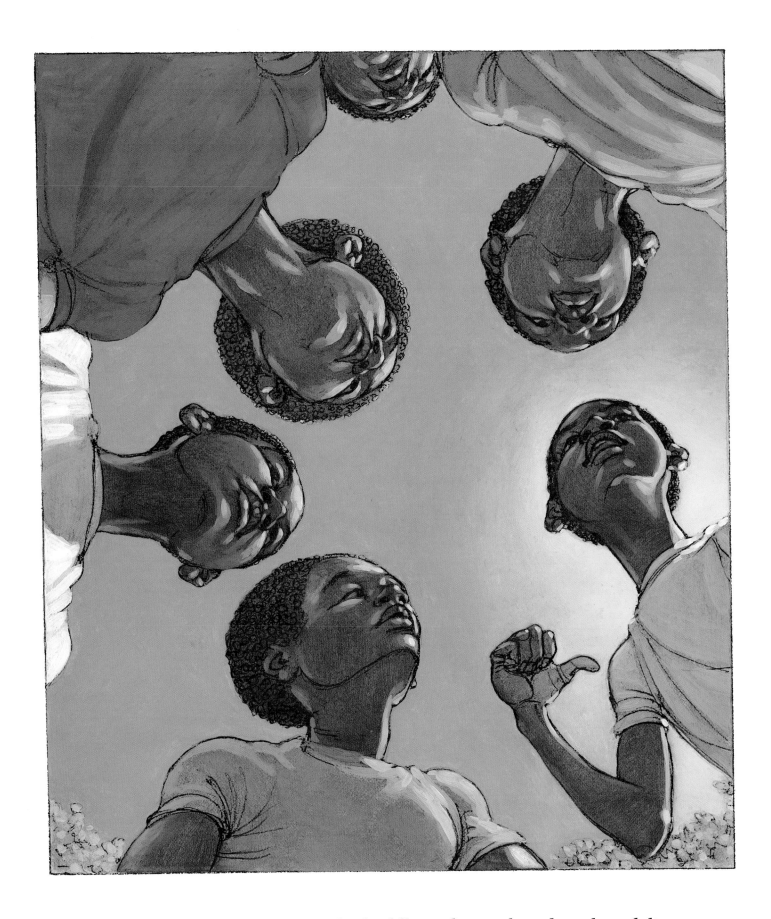

Michael joined his team in the huddle as they gathered on the sideline for a time-out.

"Okay, the game is tied. All we need is one point. Who wants to take the shot?" Ronnie asked. He looked in Michael's direction. Feeling more confident than ever, Michael said, "I'll do it."

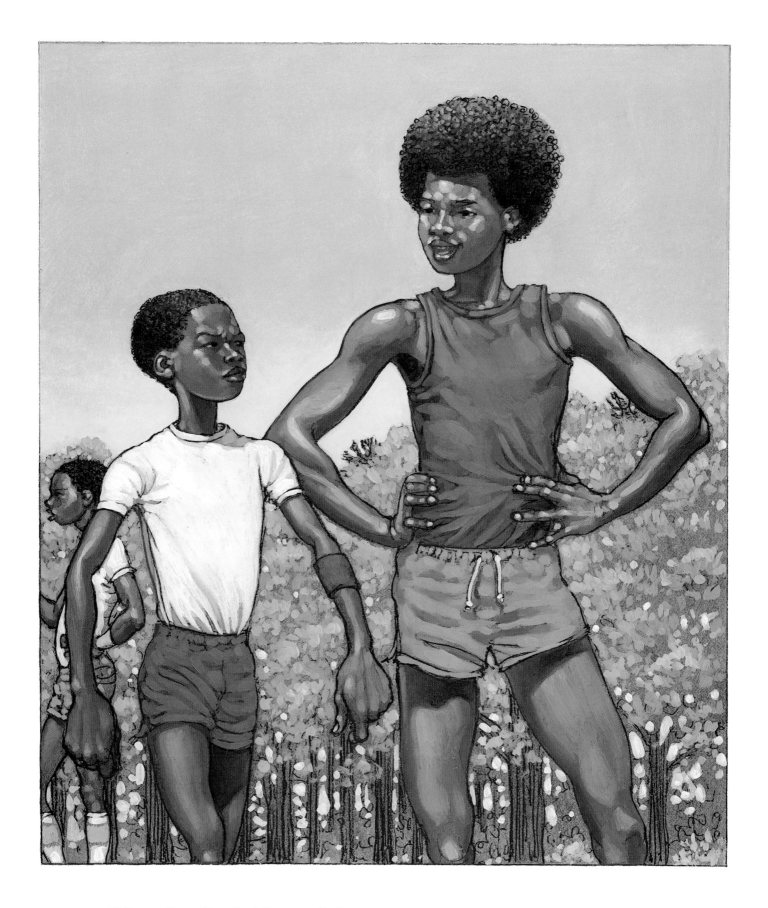

When the whistle blew and the game began again, Mark began to pick on Michael as usual.

"Still trying to play with the big boys, huh?" Mark taunted.

But Michael paid him no attention. Taller or not, he had been practicing, and today he was determined to win.

Larry threw the ball inbounds to Michael. Michael caught it, bounced it for a moment, and then took off running.

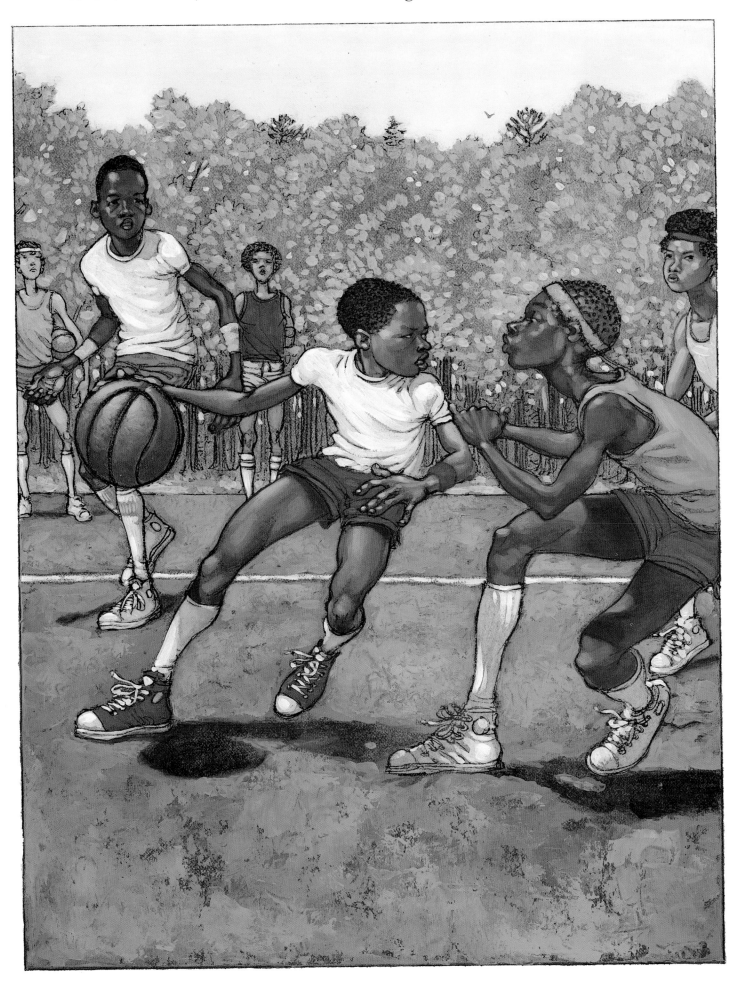

As he approached Mark, Michael shifted to his right. Mark followed, but while he was still shifting, Michael spun to his left. He stepped behind Mark and shot. The ball arced far above his opponents' hands and fell silently through the hoop. Two points! The game was over. Michael's team had won!

It was just as Michael had dreamed. When he realized what he had done, Michael took off running and didn't stop until he had reached home.

Bursting through the door, he shouted, "I did it, Daddy, I did it. I shot right over the tall guy's head and we won the game!"

Running in behind him, Ronnie and Larry joined the celebration. "That's right, little brother, you did it. You won the game for us."

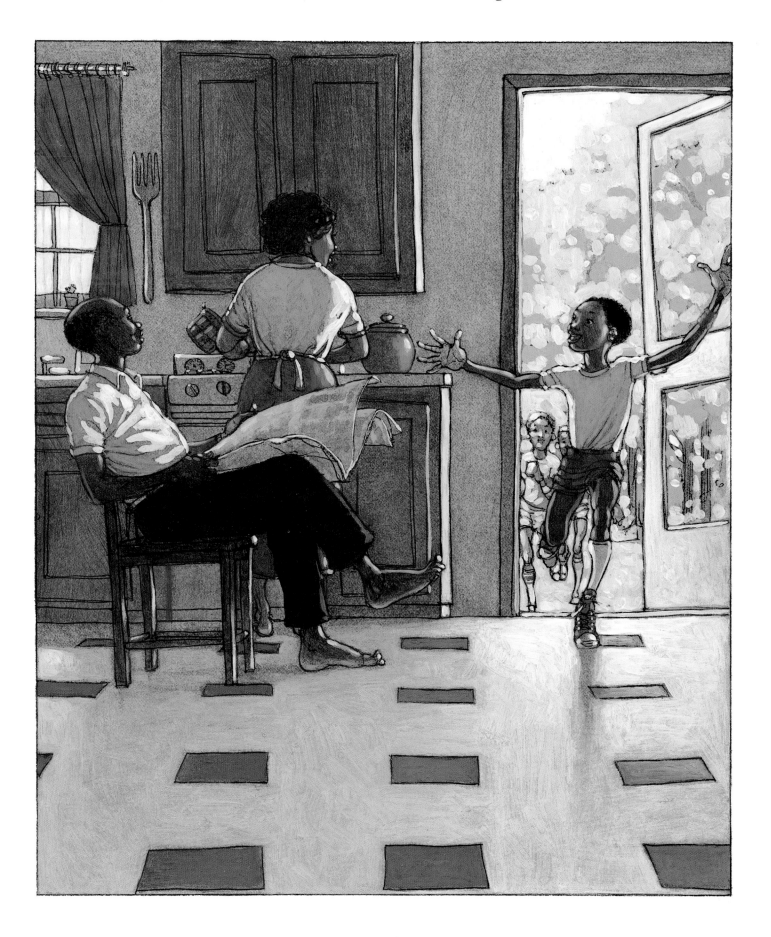

Michael remembered the look that Ronnie gave him during the last time-out of the game and said, "No, *we* won the game, but I was the star."

They all laughed.

After that day, Mama stopped putting salt in Michael's shoes, but Michael did not stop being patient and working hard and praying.

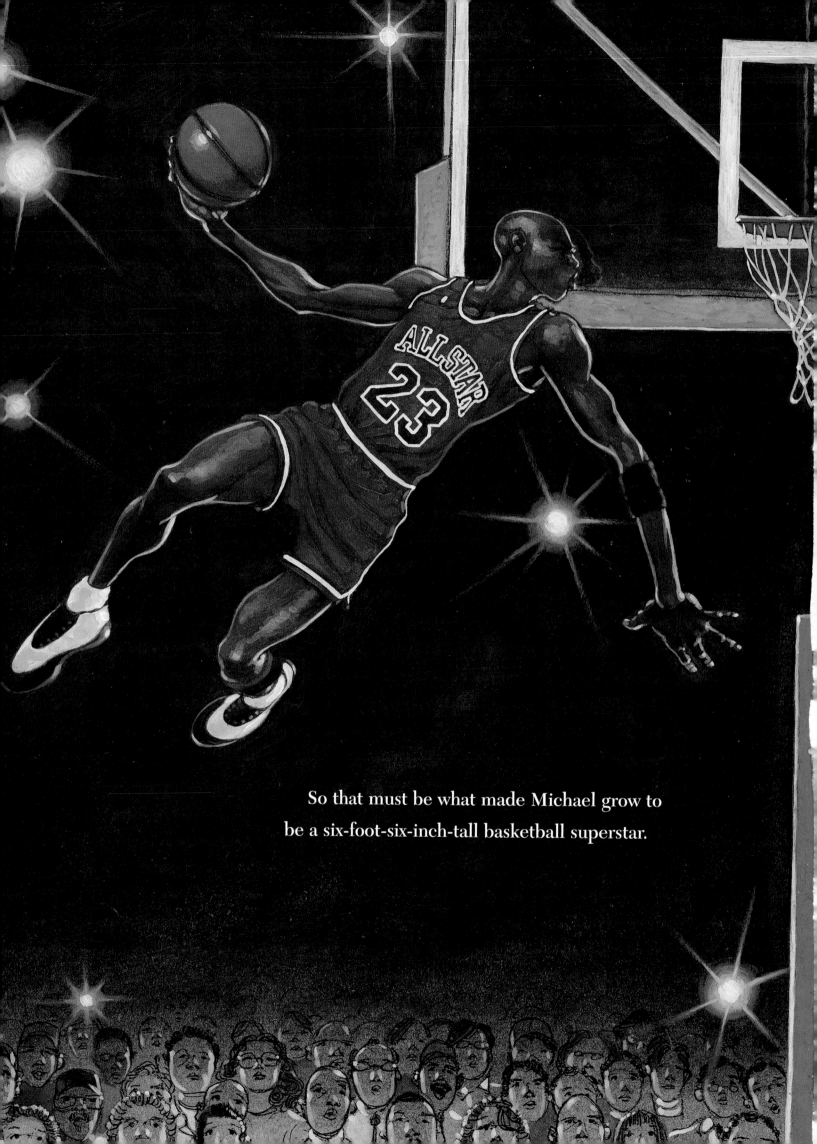

So that must be what made Michael grow to
be a six-foot-six-inch-tall basketball superstar.